Water Witcher

Little Hare Books
8/21 Mary Street, Surry Hills
NSW 2010 AUSTRALIA

www.littleharebooks.com

First published in 2006
This paperback edition first published in 2008

National Library of Australia
Cataloguing-in-Publication entry
Ormerod, Jan, 1946- .
Water witcher.

ISBN 9781921272165 (pbk).

1. Dowsing - Juvenile fiction. I. Title.

A823.3

Designed by Serious Business
Produced by Phoenix Offset, China
Printed in China through Phoenix Offset

5 4 3 2 1

Water Witcher
Jan Ormerod

LITTLE  HARE

Dougie and his sisters can't remember the last time it rained. The rainwater tanks are empty, and the creek is just a string of muddy pools. They can see the tracks of animals that come seeking water.

Everything is thirsty—the horses, the milk cow, the chickens and goats. Dougie and his sisters give sips of water to the joey and baby cockatoo.

Each day Dad and Dougie cart water from
Last Stop Well, an hour down the track.
They haul the water up bucket by bucket to fill
the tank on the dray, then bump back over the ruts,
making clouds of dust.

The crops are brown and crisp in the sun.

"It's a pity your grandfather isn't alive today," Dad says.
"He could find water for us on this very farm."

"How?" asks Dougie.

"It's called water witching," Dad explains. "He would hold a
forked stick with his palms facing upwards and elbows tucked in,
like this, and walk back and forth until the stick quivered and
pointed downwards. *It does whatever it does, no matter what I'm
thinking about,* he would say, *and that's where the water is!*
We would dig in that spot and, sure enough, we'd find clear cool
water. Your grandfather tried to teach me water witching,
but I don't have the gift. Only one in a thousand can do it."

That night, Mother dreams about gardens.
Dad dreams about fishing.
The girls dream about bubbly baths and long cool swims.
And Dougie dreams about being one in a thousand
and having the gift of water witching.

Next morning, Dougie finds a forked stick.
He holds the stick just as his grandfather had,
with his palms facing upwards and elbows tucked in,
and practises looking for water.
He walks back and forth like his dad had shown him.

"Water witcher, water witcher," tease the girls.

Dougie walks across the top paddock, along the dried-up creek,
through the vegetable garden, and around the milking shed.

He grips the forked stick and lets it do the talking.
*It has to do whatever it does, no matter what
I'm thinking about.*

What it does as he walks by the stables is quiver and
point downwards.
Has he imagined it? He tries again.
The forked stick flaps and points to the same spot each time.

"Mother, Dad," he shouts as he runs towards
the house. "Come and see!
I think I've found water!"

Dougie demonstrates, walking back and forth,
holding the forked stick delicately.
And each time he walks over that certain spot,
the stick quivers and points downwards.
"That's where the water is!" he says.
"Well," says his mother, "maybe you've found water
and maybe you haven't. All I know is that it is time for
you to help Dad fetch water from the well."
"Ah," Dad says, "let the boy dig to see what he can find."

Dougie starts to dig. He digs with all his might.
He digs until the shadows turn around at midday.
He digs and digs until the sun sets and he must stop, and still
there is no water to be seen.

That night is bath night.
First in are the cleanest, so Dougie is last of all.
His sisters tease him:
"Dirty Dougie, Dirty Dougie!"
"Dougie dug a dry well!"
He runs outside.

By the stable he sees a glimmer.
He races over to see.
His well is overflowing with fresh water!
"Quick, everyone," he cries. "I *did* find water!"

Dad and Dougie fetch the horses, and they drink their fill.
"It must be a night soak," says Dad. "Tomorrow morning the
hole will be dry, but it will be full of fresh water again
tomorrow night, and every night."

Mother and the girls look after the vegetable patch,
and every bucket and pan they can find is filled with
cool clear water for tomorrow.

Next morning, Dougie and his dad shore up the sides of
the well to stop the water flooding out each night.
Afterwards they rest in the shade, giving the joey
and the cockatoo chick a drink.
"You are one in a thousand, son," says Dad proudly.
"You are a water witcher, just like your grandfather."